Animal Tales

An

# Unexpected Arrival

Other books in the
RSPCA ANIMAL TALES series

# An Unexpected Arrival

Jess Black

RANDOM HOUSE AUSTRALIA

A Random House book
Published by Random House Australia Pty Ltd
Level 3, 100 Pacific Highway, North Sydney NSW 2060
www.randomhouse.com.au

First published by Random House Australia in 2012

Addresses for companies within the Random House Group can be
found at www.randomhouse.com.au/offices

National Library of Australia
Cataloguing-in-Publication Entry

Author: Black, Jess
Title: An unexpected arrival/Jess Black
ISBN: 978 1 74275 332 4 (pbk)
Series: Animal tales; 4
Target Audience: For primary school age
Subjects: Animals – Juvenile fiction
          Horses – Juvenile fiction
Dewey Number: A823.4

Cover photograph © Shutterstock
Cover and internal design by Ingrid Kwong
Internal illustrations by Charlotte Whitby
Internal photographs: image of cat by iStockphoto; image of horse
by Shutterstock
Typeset by Midland Typesetters, Australia
Printed in Australia by Griffin Press, an accredited ISO AS/NZS
14001:2004 Environmental Management System printer

Random House Australia uses papers that are natural, renewable and
recyclable products and made from wood grown in sustainable forests.
The logging and manufacturing processes are expected to conform to the
environmental regulations of the country of origin.

# Chapter One

Cassie Bannerman's attention was waning. It was nearing the end of the hot school day, and she stifled a yawn. As her teacher, Miss Bryan, handed out permission slips for an excursion, Cassie was only half-listening. She was busy doodling on the cover of her notebook. Cassie always drew the same horse – a bay with black mane and tail, ears pricked forward with a beautiful, friendly face. She loved to imagine owning him in real life and going on adventures together. Cassie was desperate to have her own horse one day.

'I'll need these signed by your parents and handed back in by Wednesday, please,' Miss Bryan explained as she stood at the front of the class.

Cassie looked up to see Miss Bryan holding out a form to her. She eagerly took the piece of paper from her teacher. She'd been so busy trying to get the horse's face just right that she hadn't really heard what Miss Bryan had been talking about. She studied the note. It was titled 'Spend a day at your parents' workplace.'

'Oh no!' Cassie groaned more loudly than she intended.

Miss Bryan paused and peered at Cassie over her glasses. It wasn't like Cassie to be anything but one hundred per cent enthusiastic about pretty much everything! Cassie caught her teacher's eye and immediately flashed her a bright smile. Satisfied, Miss Bryan moved on.

Cassie looked back at the form and sighed. A day at her parents' workplace. This was not exactly her dream excursion. Her folks ran the deli in Abbotts Hill and although she was happy to help out, it wasn't a novelty to see what her parents did every day to earn a living.

Miss Bryan made her way back to the front of the classroom. 'Are there any questions?' she asked just as the bell rang. Cassie's hand shot up.

The teacher smiled; here was the Cassie she knew. 'Yes, Cassie?'

'Do we *have* to spend the day with our parents?' Cassie asked tentatively.

A couple of kids laughed. Miss Bryan held up a hand to silence them, looked at Cassie and nodded.

'It's a good question, actually. Some workplaces won't be suitable for children for safety reasons, so if that is the case then those kids will have to stay at school.' She noted the look of disappointment on Cassie's face. 'Unless you can find another parent prepared to take you on.'

'Of course,' the teacher added, 'it would need to be signed off by your parents or guardian.' She looked around the room. 'That's it for the day; remember, forms have to be back to me by Wednesday.'

Students began to gather their books and bags and exit the classroom. The room was buzzing with chatter about what everyone's parents did and how exciting it would be to have a day off school.

The class bully, Adrian Cutler, nudged Cassie roughly as he pushed in front of her. 'What's the matter, Bannerman? Don't want to spend the day stuffing olives?'

Cassie's best friend, Sarah, came to her defence. 'Why don't you make like an olive and get stuffed, Adrian?'

Cassie shot Sarah an appreciative glance, turned to Adrian and glared at him before marching out of the room, leaving the bully in her tracks.

It wasn't as if Cassie didn't love her parents or respect what they did. She had years of great memories from hanging out in the deli. She just yearned to be working with her number one passion: animals.

As Cassie made her way down the hallway she caught sight of her friend Ben. He was studying the same permission slip and smiled at Cassie as she approached.

'This is awesome,' Ben exclaimed. 'We never got to do stuff like this at my old school.' He looked really excited.

'You're lucky,' said Cassie. 'Both of your parents have really interesting jobs.'

Cassie looked really downcast. Ben wasn't used to seeing her anything but her usual perky self.

'At least your parents have time to hang out with you,' he joked. 'Mine will probably be too busy and important to let me near their workplace. You know how they are.' He rolled his eyes for emphasis.

Cassie gave Ben a small smile. 'I know you're trying to cheer me up, so thanks.' She looked down at the piece of paper again, 'It's just, well, I'd give anything to swap your folks for mine, even for a day. Is that a terrible thing to say?' And without waiting for an answer, Cassie made her way outside.

Ben watched his friend go. Cassie's behaviour had really thrown him. This was a side to her he had never seen and he didn't like it. If there was a way to make Cassie smile again, then he was going to find it!

# Chapter Two

Later that night Ben was helping his mum get dinner ready by laying the table. All sorts of delicious smells were wafting into the dining room and Ben's stomach rumbled in anticipation. He wasn't the only one drawn in by the delicious smells. The family's Old English sheepdog, Florence, was lingering by the doorway to the kitchen. She'd already had her dinner, but it hadn't smelled quite as delicious as whatever Ben's mum was cooking now! She licked her lips in anticipation.

'Come on, Florence,' called Ben. 'You're in the way.' Ben nearly tripped over her as he circled the table. Ben was intrigued. It wasn't often that his mum made dinner. She was a surgeon and worked long hours at the local hospital.

'What have you cooked, Mum?' asked Ben as he grabbed a handful of knives and forks. 'Let me guess, spaghetti and meatballs?' It was his mum's signature and only dish.

'Ha ha!' laughed Veronica sarcastically. 'Actually, I had spare time today, so I tried something new, something quite special. I bet you'll have seconds, and dessert.'

'You've made dessert?' Ben grabbed the dining room chair for support as he pretended to almost faint in surprise.

Veronica rolled her eyes. 'You won't get any at this rate! Do me a favour and tell your father that dinner's ready.'

'Dad!' yelled Ben as he continued to lay out the cutlery.

'ARF!' barked Florence as she too called Dr Joe. She knew this game. Soon they would all be eating, which meant that she would be available to hoover up any scraps that might fall on the floor!

His mum winced. 'I meant that you should leave the room and get him,

11

not perforate my eardrum. You too, Florence. Out!'

Just then Ben's dad wandered into the dining room and broke into a huge smile when he saw his wife placing bowls of delicious-smelling food on the table. He gave Florence a friendly tickle behind her ear and took a seat. 'Fantastic! I'm starving.'

Dr Joe surveyed the feast before him. 'Did you make this, love?' he asked, trying to keep the surprise from his voice as he helped himself to a serving.

Veronica chose to ignore her husband's question and turned to her son. 'What did you get up to at school today, Ben?'

Ben played thoughtfully with a strand of creamy fettuccine. He couldn't stop thinking about Cassie.

'Earth to Ben! Come in, Ben!' said Veronica as she good-naturedly ruffled Ben's hair. 'Hey, space cadet, I finally make it home for dinner and you're a world away.'

Ben smiled. 'Sorry, Mum, I didn't hear you. What did you say?'

Through a creamy mouthful of food, Dr Joe pointed in delight to the meal in front of him. 'This is actually really, really good!'

Veronica again ignored him and turned her attention back to Ben. 'I was wondering if anything interesting happened at school today.'

Ben put down his fork and looked at his mum. 'Well, we have to spend a day at our parents' workplace.' He dug out the permission slip from his jeans pocket and handed the crumpled note to his mother.

Veronica read it and passed it across the table to her husband. 'That's fantastic. We can spend the whole day together. I can introduce you to all the heads of department at the hospital; it'll be so much fun!'

Ben cut his mother off before she could get any further. 'Actually, Mum, I hope you don't mind, but I was hoping to spend the day with Dad.'

Veronica couldn't keep the disappointment from her face. 'I get it. It's a guy thing?'

'It's a Cassie thing.' Ben explained further. 'You both know how much she loves animals. She spends enough time in the deli as it is. I think she'd love to see a real vet at work.'

'There's a reason they've won best local delicatessen for the last three years running. Those Bannermans can cook!' exclaimed Dr Joe, while helping himself to seconds. He turned to his wife. 'Who knew that you could cook, too? Love, you've outdone yourself. This is delicious!'

Veronica looked down at the table sheepishly. 'Well, when I said I made it . . .'

But Dr Joe was only half-listening. 'Ben, I've got a field trip coming up that would be perfect for you. I need to go out to a local farm and assess them for the RSPCA. Cassie is welcome to join us.'

Ben's eyes lit up. 'Really? Thanks, Dad!' He turned to his mother. 'Mum, can I be excused to ring Cassie and tell her?'

Veronica sighed. 'Sure, love.'

After Ben had left the room, Dr Joe eyed the pasta with the excitement of a man who didn't often get a home-cooked meal. 'You'll have to talk me through how you made this. I want to know how you got the carbonara so creamy.' He looked up. 'Exactly how long did you simmer the sauce for?'

Veronica put her fork down on the table with a clatter. 'Okay, okay, I confess, Your Honour. I didn't make it myself; I picked it up from the Bannermans' on the way home!'

Dr Joe smiled and took her hand. He didn't look terribly surprised by the confession. 'Sweetheart, you don't need to pretend. We love you even though you're a terrible cook.' He held up his fork in emphasis as he continued, 'And those Bannermans, they can really cook.'

Veronica sighed and took a mouthful of fettuccine. Her husband was right – it was really very good! She smiled. 'Wait till you try their dessert!'

# Chapter Three

The morning of the school excursion arrived. Cassie's parents had happily given her permission to spend the day with Dr Joe on official RSPCA duty. They knew full well how much it would mean to Cassie to go out to a farm and see Dr Joe in action.

At 8 am sharp, Cassie watched as Ben and his dad pulled up outside her house. Dr Joe was driving a vehicle that displayed the RSPCA logo proudly on both sides of the car. Cassie was so excited to be travelling in it!

'We're in the paw mobile,' she squealed as she strapped herself into her seatbelt. 'This is so cool!'

Ben and Joe exchanged a look. Dr Joe cleared his throat and turned to Cassie. 'Good to have you with us, Cassie.'

'Thanks, Dr Joe,' chirped Cassie. 'I'm really excited. I've even done some research into chicken and egg farming. For instance, did you know that scientists think the closest living relative to the Tyrannosaurus Rex is a chicken?'

Dr Joe met Cassie's eyes through the rear-view mirror. 'Can't say I knew that, Cassie.' He smiled to himself as he started the engine.

'Speaking of chickens . . .' piped up Ben, determined to match Cassie in the chicken stakes. 'Why did the chicken cross the playground?'

She shrugged.

'To get to the other slide,' answered Ben, laughing heartily at his own joke.

Cassie rolled her eyes. 'Did you know that it takes about twenty-one days for an egg to hatch?'

'Why did the chicken cross the road back again?' asked Ben.

Dr Joe shook his head. 'I don't know. Why?'

'Because he was a double-crosser.' Ben snorted and soon they were all chuckling.

Before too long they were out on the open road as the scenery provided more and more open space and farm animals and less dense housing. They travelled for some time in silence, each taking in the view of the country as they gradually left the city behind.

'I should probably fill you kids in on what today is all about.' Dr Joe glanced through his rear-view mirror at the two expectant faces in the back seat. 'Well, the RSPCA encourages farmers to improve farming practices to ensure the animals are more comfortable and can live a happy life. So they have introduced the Approved

Farming Scheme, and farms that provide high welfare standards for their animals can join the Scheme.'

Cassie's eyes lit up and she held up a hand excitedly. Dr Joe chuckled. 'We're not in school now, Cassie. You can speak without raising your hand.'

Cassie exclaimed. 'I've seen them. My folks sell eggs in the deli that are RSPCA approved.'

'That's right. They would be stamped with the paw of approval,' agreed Dr Joe. 'If farmers meet the standards that the RSPCA lay out, then their products will be given the Paw of Approval and the RSPCA will endorse their products.'

'The Paw of Approval,' breathed Cassie in awe. 'That's brilliant.'

'Next time you're in the supermarket or butcher, have a look for the paw. Research shows that most Australians are interested in buying products from farmers who look after their animals properly.'

'That makes sense,' Ben said, nodding his head. 'So what will you be looking for today?'

'This farm has hens, which lay eggs that are sold commercially. We call them "layer hens". I have a checklist of things that those animals need to be able to do and eat in order to pass.' He made a right-hand turn down a dirt road. 'We're nearly there, kids. It might be a little boring, okay? There's heaps of paperwork to be done.'

Cassie gazed out of the car window at the huge farm and its open paddocks, which reached as far as her eyes could see. 'Bored? Right now I could be making my own body weight in potato salad. Believe me, I won't be bored.'

# Chapter Four

Dr Joe pulled the paw mobile to a halt outside a pretty farmhouse that was nestled among a patch of tall pine trees. Here they were at Brackenridge Farm. The house was a plain weatherboard, but someone had taken great care with the garden; colourful flowers in pots adorned the pathway and entrance.

While Dr Joe got his paperwork together Cassie noticed two figures sitting on the timber deck, which wrapped around the outside of the house. An older man was seated next to a teenage boy. They both stood and approached the car.

The older man definitely looked like a farmer. He wore a short-sleeve collared shirt and faded pants with brown leather boots. He also wore a cap on his head. His skin was tanned from prolonged exposure to the sun. He looked strong but open and friendly.

The boy wore similar clothes, except he wore sneakers instead of boots and his hair was dark brown and longer. It stuck out in wisps from under his cap.

Dr Joe glanced back to Cassie and Ben as he gathered his clipboard and paperwork. 'Let's get to work, kids!'

Cassie could hardly contain her excitement as she stepped out of the car. Here she was on a real working farm with a vet, being given the opportunity to see if the animals were well looked after. It didn't get much better than that!

'Welcome,' said the farmer as he shook Dr Joe's hand. 'I'm David, and this is my son, Steve.'

'Nice to meet you both,' greeted Dr Joe warmly.

'G'day', said Steve as he cleared his throat.

David turned to greet Ben and Cassie with a smile. 'And I heard we'd be having some extra guests today.'

Ben held out a hand. 'I'm Ben, and this is Cassie.'

David smiled at Cassie. 'Are you brother and sister?'

Ben looked momentarily horrified at the idea but then laughed. 'Ah, no, we're, um, at the same school.' He blushed. 'I mean, we're friends. Our school sent us out to spend a day at our parents' work.' He pointed to Dr Joe. 'He's my dad.'

'And?' David turned questioningly to Cassie.

'My folks run a deli,' said Cassie.

'Ah, and you'd rather spend the day outdoors?' asked David.

Cassie nodded.

He gave Cassie a wink. 'Me too.'

Dr Joe, Cassie and Ben took a few moments to put on special boot covers and change into clean overalls to avoid any risk of contamination.

David turned to Dr Joe, who was studying his paperwork. 'It's good to have you here, Joe. My father was an egg farmer and I've changed the place pretty radically since I took over management of the farm. As far as I'm concerned our animals are our livelihood. If we expect to earn a living from them, then we owe them a good life. I'm always interested in making improvements, so if you have suggestions for me, I'm all ears.'

'We have a checking system we need to go through. It's a little time-consuming.

How about we start with the hens?' suggested Dr Joe.

David nodded. 'Come with me.' He turned to the kids as he led the way. 'Have either of you two ever seen a battery hen farm?'

Cassie and Ben shook their heads.

David continued, 'I guess you wouldn't have had the chance, being from the city. It's certainly a memory you'll never forget. The chickens live their whole lives in cages. To me, that's more like a factory than a farm.'

'Sounds horrible.' Ben shuddered.

'It is. The difference between a battery hen farm and our place is that our hens get to run around as nature intended. Hens like to scratch in the dirt, perch and forage. They are also social creatures, so they like to mix with other hens and have a chat.'

While they walked, Cassie noticed that Brackenridge looked clean and uncluttered. The farm was well loved.

As they turned a corner Cassie was struck by a loud noise. In front of them, as far as they could see, were hundreds of hens roaming about freely and boy, they really did like chatting. Those birds were a noisy bunch!

Steve went ahead and unlocked a large metal swing gate. He held it open for them all to walk through.

'You won't see any cages here,' pointed out David. 'The hens can move freely inside and outdoors, and they can lay their eggs in nests.'

Dr Joe was busy taking notes. Cassie looked around at the hens. They really did seem to be happy. And why not, with such pleasant living conditions. Some were pecking at feed, others were squawking while some just sat on perches and watched the world go by.

# Chapter Five

Dr Joe was satisfied he had seen everything he needed to in order to complete his assessment of the hens and their living conditions. As they left the hen paddock, Dr Joe walked with David and Cassie while Steve and Ben fell into conversation about the rugby.

Cassie felt as if she was being watched. She turned around to discover a sleek border collie trotting behind her. The dog walked stiffly. Cassie could tell she was an old dog, but her coat was shiny, her nose looked wet and her eyes were clear and bright.

'Hello, and who are you?' she asked the border collie.

David glanced back and gave the dog a dismissive wave. 'Don't mind Tess. She's an old nosey parker. Loves to know what's going on around the farm, but she'll probably keep her distance. She's pretty picky with newcomers.'

As if she had understood every word and disagreed with the assessment, Tess sauntered up to Cassie's outstretched palm and not only gave her a good sniff, but gave Cassie's hand a generous lick to boot!

'Well, I never,' commented David, genuinely surprised.

Cassie leaned over and gave the old dog a decent tickle behind her ear.

In turn, Tess lifted her paw and placed it on Cassie's knee.

'Now that's a first,' exclaimed Steve.

Ben rolled his eyes and laughed. 'That's Cassie. Without even trying, she's been given the paw of approval!'

'If only it was as easy for us!' David laughed as the group continued on back to the farmhouse.

'You're so lucky you get to live out in the country,' Cassie spoke to Tess as the two brought up the rear. 'Ripper would love it out here.' It didn't seem at all unusual for Cassie to chat to animals. She knew that they might not understand every word, but they got the general gist of her conversation.

Tess looked around at her surroundings as if giving the farm a familiar once-over. There wasn't much that went on at Brackenridge that Tess didn't know about. She paused, cocked her head as her ears pricked up and she gave a low growl.

'What is it, girl?' Cassie asked the dog.

Cassie turned to see what had caught Tess's attention. In a paddock a little distance away stood three horses resting under the shade of a drooping willow. One lazily swatted a fly with its tail, another was grazing slowly; the third horse looked

to be asleep in the hot sun, eyelids drooping.

'Horses!' Cassie's excitement got the better of her and she spoke more loudly than she'd intended. In her enthusiasm she forgot Tess's warning growl as she pointed to the horses so Ben could see them too.

Ben took the hint and nudged Steve. 'Can you tell that Cassie likes horses?'

Steve crossed his arms across his chest. 'Have the RSPCA got you on the payroll yet, Cassie?'

Cassie blushed and looked at the ground. 'No, I'm too young.'

'Plenty of time,' said Steve with a smile. He couldn't help but notice the way Cassie was gazing at the horses in the distance. 'Come on, they could do with a carrot or two. We'll catch up with Dad in a minute.'

Steve wandered over to a stables area. He came back with a handful of carrots and gave a few to both Ben and Cassie. Then he let out a loud whistle.

'They'll meet us at the fence by the water trough.' Steve pointed to an area where the grass had long since worn away to dirt. 'This is where they're normally fed at night.'

Following Steve's lead, Ben and Cassie clambered up the wooden fence and swung their legs over the other side, sitting comfortably on the top rail. The horses ambled over lazily to see what these newcomers had to offer.

'How long have you lived here, Steve?' asked Cassie.

'All my life. It's all I've ever known,' explained Steve. 'Things were different around here when I was little. My grand-father ran the farm and there were no free-ranging animals then. Dad was determined to change the way things were done. Some of the staff we took on didn't approve, but Dad found people who, like us, cared about how animals were treated. He wanted to feel proud of his farm and to know that the welfare of the animals came first.'

'Good for him,' said Ben.

'Yeah, well, it hasn't been easy. That's why this approval from the RSPCA is so important to the business.' Steve gave one of the horses a pat as she ambled over to him. She stretched out her head and her bottom lip quivered as she felt around his hands for the carrot she could smell.

'Hold the palm of your hand out flat with the carrot lying on top,' explained Steve.

Ben and Cassie did as they were told and the horses munched and crunched appreciatively.

Cassie watched as the horses' big teeth snapped through the carrot with ease. They were such large muscular creatures. How lucky humans were to be able to hop onto their back and run like the wind.

Ben noticed another horse way off in the distance beside another patch of trees. 'How come that fella hasn't come over for some morning tea?' he asked Steve.

Steve shielded his eyes from the sun as he squinted down to the border of the paddock. 'Piper? Not like her to miss a snack and some company.' He was about to let out another shrill whistle to get the horse's attention when they heard David's voice calling them to come and help.

'Oops. Forgot we're meant to be working. Come on!' Steve gave the horse he had been feeding one last pat and jumped down from the fence.

He held out a hand for Cassie. She gave the horses another lingering look but then reminded herself they were here to work after all. She and Ben joined Steve and they hurried over to meet David and Dr Joe.

In her haste, Cassie forgot about Tess. She didn't notice the border collie slip out into the paddock, looking very much like a dog on a mission.

# Chapter Six

Having spent enough time on the farm to complete his checklist, Dr Joe seemed satisfied enough to end the formal part of the farm inspection. He and David headed back to the farmhouse to get some lunch together and continue their conversation.

David allowed Ben and Cassie to have a look around the surrounding paddocks with the promise that they would be careful not to disturb any animals. They soon found themselves wandering back to look at the horses.

While Cassie chatted to the three horses they had fed earlier that morning, Ben's attention was distracted once again by the lone horse further down in the paddock near the fence perimeter.

'Hey, Cassie.' Ben pointed to the horse. 'Check out that horse. Do you think there's something wrong with her?'

Cassie looked over and could see Piper pawing the ground. She seemed to be very restless and unsettled, walking around and around in circles, flicking her tail. Cassie heard a dog bark in the distance and then realised that Tess was near the horse.

'Tess looks anxious,' noted Cassie.

'Let's go take a closer look,' said Ben as he slipped between two wooden rails in the fence.

'We weren't meant to disturb the animals, remember?' cautioned Cassie.

'If there's something wrong with the horse, we should check it out,' said Ben.

Cassie nodded. He was right and she was interested to see what had both animals so excited.

It was a large paddock and they were both puffing by the time they drew closer to the two animals. They slowed down and walked calmly as they approached the horse. Piper was just like Cassie's dream horse, a true bay in colour with black mane and tail. Right now, however, her brown coat was stained almost black with sweat and she was breathing heavily. From up close it was obvious that something was wrong.

'Don't go too close to her,' warned Ben. 'She's not happy.' She was flicking her tail in a very agitated manner.

'She looks really uncomfortable,' said Cassie in a low voice. 'I think we should get your dad. She might be in pain.'

Ben nodded. 'It could be colic.'

The horse's back was arched and she let out a deep groan. Tess grew more agitated and let out a series of shrill barks.

'I think Tess is trying to tell us something!' cried Cassie.

'Let's go!' Ben took off at a jog with Cassie following behind. 'We better get Dad, and fast!'

Cassie and Ben burst inside to find Dr Joe and David shaking hands while Steve was beaming from ear to ear.

'Ah, kids, you're just in time to congratulate David. I'll be recommending that David's farm becomes an RSPCA-approved farm. It definitely meets the RSPCA standards,' said Dr Joe.

'That's fantastic,' spluttered Ben. 'The only problem is we think your horse Piper might be sick!'

'Why do you say that?' asked David, his smile fading.

'She's acting really strangely,' explained Ben.

'Pawing the ground, restless and sweating,' chimed in Cassie. 'Ben said it could be colic. That's really serious, isn't it?'

David exhaled deeply. 'I can't believe I haven't kept a closer eye on her. We got so caught up with the inspection that Steve and I have been really distracted.'

At that moment the penny dropped for Steve. 'I can't believe I didn't put two and two together when we saw her earlier!' he gasped. 'Piper's not sick. She's foaling!'

54

When he saw the blank look on Cassie's face he explained further. 'Foaling means Piper's in labour. She's going to have a baby!'

# Chapter Seven

Dr Joe grabbed his medical kit and hurried down to the paddock to join the small group as they made their way to where Piper was kept.

They scanned the paddock, but Piper was nowhere to be seen.

'Where is she?' cried Cassie as they ran through the paddock to where they had last seen the horse.

'Horses like to give birth alone and often wander off,' panted Dr Joe. He strode through the long grass to catch up to the others.

'How big is this paddock?' asked Cassie.

'It's not that big,' said Steve. 'She's probably wandered down to the creek.' His eyes widened. 'Unless . . .'

'Unless?' repeated Dr Joe. He was getting anxious about the welfare of his patient.

'Well, if the gate to the big paddock was left open, she has acres and acres of land to have wandered off into,' added David.

58

'Only one way to find out!' called Ben as he began running towards the creek bed.

The others followed. Cassie was beginning to worry about the mare who had been in such distress when they had last set eyes on her. If only she had stayed with her and sent Ben for help. At least then she wouldn't be alone.

Cassie's love affair with horses had led her to read many books about horse and pony care. She knew that lots of things could go wrong with the birth of a foal. It was much safer to have a vet present when it happened!

They crossed the creek and made their way up the bank on the other side, only to find that what Steve had feared had happened. The gate was wide open.

Steve bent over with his hands on his knees to catch his breath. 'This paddock is massive. She could be anywhere!'

David tried to remain calm. 'Maybe if we split up into small groups?' he suggested.

'I've got an idea!' cried Cassie.

Dr Joe knew enough to take Cassie seriously when it came to an animals' wellbeing. 'We're all ears, Cassie.'

'Tess was with her when we last saw her. It was Tess who tried to tell us something was wrong. If we can find Tess we can find Piper!' she urged.

'Okay,' said David. 'Let's try it.' He let out a loud wolf-whistle while Steve began calling out to Tess.

'Here, girl! Tess!' cried Cassie.

Soon everyone was shouting out the dog's name. Suddenly David held up a hand to silence the others. 'I think I can hear her.'

He was right. In the distance they could hear the faint sound of a dog barking.

'That's Tess, all right,' said Steve.

The group took off at a jog and by following the sound of Tess's urgent barks they soon came across the horse. Tess was racing around in circles, barking madly.

'No wonder we couldn't see her!' exclaimed Dr Joe.

Piper was lying down and was almost completely hidden by the long grass.

'Well done, Tess!' said Cassie as she gave the old dog a big cuddle. 'We wouldn't have found Piper without you!'

Meanwhile Dr Joe had wasted no time in giving the mare a quick look-over. 'There's no time to lose. The labour has progressed to second stage and it's my guess that Piper needs help immediately.'

# Chapter Eight

The ache in Ben's arms and legs was really starting to set in. He and Cassie had already done three trips back and forth from the house to where Piper lay in the far paddock, bringing towels and linen and more equipment for Dr Joe from the paw mobile. On this trip they were carrying a heavy bucket between them filled with hot water.

'Need to rest.' Ben motioned for Cassie to put the bucket down so he could take a break.

'Oh,' he groaned as he rubbed his hands together. 'Farming is hard work, I'm not sure I'm cut out for it.'

'Come on, Ben!' said Cassie a little impatiently. 'Your dad needs this water in order to properly disinfect. Piper needs our help!'

Ben again picked up the bucket and grimaced. The handle was cutting into his hands and he felt lightheaded from being out in the hot sun, but he gritted his teeth and pushed on. After all, if Cassie could do it then so could he!

'I swear this bucket is getting heavier by the minute,' he muttered.

As they approached the horse they could see that Dr Joe had taken off his shirt and was disinfecting his hands and arms. He needed to feel around inside Piper to see if the foal was facing the right way for the mare to give birth without difficulty.

Steve and David had tied Piper's hind legs together with twine so that she wouldn't kick Dr Joe.

'Well done. You kids have been really helpful,' said Dr Joe. He used the water to wash his hands and arms thoroughly. 'Stand back now, just in case.'

Cassie couldn't believe she was watching a vet in action on a real farm. Although many modern farms used quad bikes and motorbikes, David still kept a few horses. Piper's foal would grow up on the farm as a working horse, just like Piper. While David and Steve held Piper still, Dr Joe gave her a physical examination.

Cassie, Ben and Tess sat alongside each other, watching in silence.

'It sure is mucky work being a vet,' whispered Cassie to Ben, as they watched Dr Joe's entire arm disappear into the horse.

'You should hear my mum grumble,' Ben whispered back. 'Dad's work clothes always need a double wash!'

Once Dr Joe was finished he soaped his arms once again. He looked troubled. Tess let out a loud bark as if to ask him what was wrong. Hurry up, people, she seemed to be saying – let's get this foal out into the world!

'I hear you, Tess,' soothed Dr Joe. He turned to the others. 'I had hoped to feel the foal's legs, but all I seem to get a hold of is the head.'

'What does that mean, Dr Joe?' asked Cassie.

'It means we need to try and get the foal to turn around so Piper can give birth to her foal, front legs first,' explained Dr Joe.

'How do we do that?' asked Ben.

Dr Joe studied the horse. 'Can you untie her legs, Steve?' he asked. 'We're going to need to get her to stand up and walk around. It might help shift the position of the foal.'

David looked warily at Ben and Cassie, who were both awestruck by the scene unfolding in front of them. 'Are you kids up for some hard yakka?'

Cassie leapt to her feet, her green eyes shining. 'I thought you'd never ask!'

# Chapter Nine

Time seemed to stand still. Cassie and Ben couldn't have said if they were in the paddock with Piper for thirty minutes or three hours. They were so focused on helping the mare and Dr Joe that they could think of little else. If someone had asked either of them their name, they may have had trouble remembering!

'Go, Piper, you can do it!' Cassie chanted under her breath, over and over again. She was so nervous and excited about the foal being born.

Ben stood next to his dad, lending a hand in any way he could. This sure beat a day sitting in a classroom!

With effort they had managed to get Piper to stand and walk around in order to try to shift the position of the foal.

Then they had to get her to lie down again in order for Dr Joe to give her another inspection. He was now able to manipulate the position of the foal so that its front feet were forward.

Now it was left to Piper to let nature take its course. Her contractions were coming thick and fast and the horse was working hard, grunting and groaning with each one.

'We're nearly there,' said Dr Joe in a low voice, encouraging Piper with regular strokes on her flank. All of a sudden out popped a small hoof covered in white fluid, which was soon followed by another hoof.

'Wowzer!' Cassie gasped. A foal was being born right in front of her eyes! She stared, entranced, as two long spindly legs followed the hooves and out slid the foal's head.

With one last contraction the head was followed by shoulders and a body, until finally the foal came out with a 'whoosh' and slid to the ground. It didn't look like any foal Cassie had ever seen. It was covered in all sorts of slime.

'Well done, Piper!' said David, giving the mare a gentle pat on the neck.

'Way to go, Piper!' called Steve.

Even Tess gave a low *woof* and wagged her tail happily in appreciation of the mare's efforts.

While Dr Joe and David got busy cleaning the area on the foal where the umbilical cord had been, Cassie and Ben gave each other a high five.

'Congratulations!' said Dr Joe to David. 'You have a beautiful new female foal.'

'Thanks to you, Joe!' David smiled. 'It was a good thing you were here.'

They watched as the weary new mother turned to sniff her new baby and then begin to lick her clean.

'That was amazing, Dad!' Ben stared at his father with pride.

Dr Joe smiled as he buttoned his shirt back on. 'Well, I couldn't let you down on "Spend a day at your parents' work", could I? Had to pull something dramatic out of my hat.'

'I just wished you'd given us a clue first!' joked Steve.

They started to pack up the equipment.

'Do we really have to go now?' asked Cassie.

'I will have to take you home eventually, Cass, or your parents will ask questions!' Dr Joe checked his watch. 'But we still have some paperwork to finish up, so you can stay here for a bit longer.'

'Yay!' cried Ben and Cassie in unison.

They watched as the spindly-legged foal slowly and clumsily staggered to her feet to take a first feed from Piper. Soon she was suckling noisily.

'Which reminds me,' said Dr Joe. 'We never had lunch, I'm starving!'

All too soon it was time to say goodbye. David and Steve stood in the driveway to wave them off. Just as Cass was about to get into the paw mobile, she paused.

'You know,' said Cassie, 'I've realised that my parents might run a deli but they can make a difference too. If the farmer makes a change and the customer makes a change, then it's also up to the person who sells the goods to make a change to what they stock in their shop.'

'Exactly!' said Ben. 'I mean, I'm happy for your parents of course, but the amount of meals we buy from your shop means we'll be supporting the RSPCA too!'

Dr Joe chuckled. 'Don't I know it!'

'See you later,' David and Steve called out. Cassie and Ben waved goodbye to them as they got in the car.

'Bye, Tess,' said Cassie. 'Take care of Piper and the new foal for me.'

Tess gave a happy bark in response. She was definitely going to keep an eye on the farm's newest arrival!

**RSPCA**

## ABOUT THE RSPCA

The RSPCA is the country's best known and most respected animal welfare organisation. The first RSPCA in Australia was formed in Victoria in 1871, and the organisation is now represented by RSPCAs in every state and territory.

The RSPCA's mission is to prevent cruelty to animals by actively promoting their care and protection. It is a not-for-profit charity that is firmly based in the Australian community, relying upon the support of individuals, businesses and organisations to survive and continue its vital work.

Every year, RSPCA shelters throughout Australia accept over 150,000 sick, injured or abandoned animals from the community. The RSPCA believes that every animal is entitled to the Five Freedoms:

# Fact File

- freedom from hunger and thirst (ready access to fresh water and a healthy, balanced diet)
- freedom from discomfort, including accommodation in an appropriate environment that has shelter and a comfortable resting area
- freedom from pain, injury or disease through prevention or rapid diagnosis and providing veterinary treatment when required

- freedom to express normal behaviour, including sufficient space, proper facilities and company of the animal's own kind and
- freedom from fear and distress through conditions and treatment that avoid suffering.

# EGGS YOU CAN TRUST: RSPCA

The RSPCA has developed animal welfare standards for the care of layer hens, pigs, meat chickens and turkeys. The standards ensure that animals in these farming systems are provided with an environment that meets their behavioural and physiological needs.

In the case of layer hens, the RSPCA logo can be found on both barn-laid and free-range eggs that have been produced according to the RSPCA's Approved Farming

# Fact File

Scheme Standards. People who buy eggs carrying the RSPCA logo can trust that hens are treated to the RSPCA's high animal-welfare standards on farm.

Consumers should make sure the eggs they buy are certified by a trustworthy and independent authority, like the RSPCA.

RSPCA-approved eggs are a great choice because the farms that produce these eggs undergo stringent and regular assessment processes to ensure the RSPCA Approved Farming Scheme's strict welfare standards are being met.

The RSPCA encourages more farmers to join the RSPCA Approved Farming Scheme.

Just look for the RSPCA Paw of Approval on the egg carton.

# Fact File

## What constitutes free-range?

The RSPCA believes a proper free-range environment should provide hens with sufficient space to express their natural behaviours, and that all hens should have access to the range for at least eight hours each day.

Access to the outdoors should be easy for hens, through good-sized openings or pop holes; the outdoor area should have lots of space and palatable vegetation for foraging, as well as adequate shelter and secure fences to keep out foxes, rodents and other predators.

Pictures on egg cartons don't necessarily reflect how eggs were produced. So to be sure consumers are getting what they pay for, they should check that the eggs they are purchasing are audited against publicly available standards.

# Fact File

These standards should include details of all of the aspects on farm, for example, how much space hens are allocated inside and outside the shed, what environmental enrichment hens are given, the suitability of the range area, including the range size and protection, and how frequently the farms are inspected against the standards.

What's needed most is a nationally consistent legal definition of the term 'free range' and other such terms used to describe different production systems of animals, especially terms that imply improved animal welfare. Tighter regulation of the industry itself is also needed so consumers can be sure that their choices in the egg aisle will have a positive impact on hen welfare.

RSPCA ❤❤

# RSPCA-APPROVED FARMING

RSPCA-approved farms are farms that produce animal products to the RSPCA's high animal-welfare standards.

The RSPCA has been working with farmers by encouraging welfare-friendly farming practices since the mid-90s. The RSPCA first worked with layer hen and pig farmers, and in 2010 the Approved Farming Scheme expanded to include standards for meat, chicken and turkey farmers.

Over the past five years, consumer awareness about higher welfare food has grown rapidly with more people questioning where their food comes from and how it's been produced.

## Fact File

RSPCA-approved products can be found by visiting www.shophumane.org.au. Egg, pork, chicken and turkey that are RSPCA approved have been produced to animal welfare standards much higher than required by law or the relevant model codes of practice.